WALT DISNEY'S

Bambi Gets Lost

text by Albert G. Miller

Random House　New York

Library of Congress Cataloging in Publication Data

Miller, Albert G. 1905- Bambi gets lost.

Bambi and Thumper get lost in the woods and must ask directions several times.

[1. Stories in rhyme] I. Bambi (Motion picture) II. Title.
PZ8.3.M612Bam 811'.5'4 [E] 72-4859 ISBN 0-394-82520-9
ISBN 0-394-92520-3 (lib. bdg.)

Manufactured in the United States of America

F G H I J K

0 1 2 3 4 5 6 7 8 9

"Hi, Bambi," said Thumper. "I hopped in to say
That this is a wonderful morning to play."

He found Bambi's mother, and said, "Will you please
Let Bambi come play with me under the trees?"
"Yes, but stay very close to home while you play,
Because you'll get lost if you go far away."

"Oh, boy!" shouted Bambi. "We're going to have fun!"
"You said it," cried Thumper. "Come, Bambi, let's run!"

Forgetting what Bambi's wise mother had said,
They soon left the path for the hill far ahead.

They came to the hilltop, and what did they see?
Two cute little bear cubs, way up in a tree.
The bears were good climbers because they had claws,
Like those on the ends of a pussycat's paws.

Right close to where Bambi and Thumper were standing
A nice, friendly bird glided in for a landing.

"If I had two wings," Thumper told him, "I'd fly.
And then we could race through the clouds in the sky."

The bird looked surprised. "Now that would be funny.
Imagine two wings on the back of a bunny!"

"Say, Thumper," said Bambi. "We've come pretty far.
I think we are lost—do you know where we are?"
"Why, sure," Thumper said. "Don't you worry—you'll see!
I'll get us home safely. Just leave it to me."

When Bambi bent over to smell a pink rose,
He saw something yellow in front of his nose.

"You must be a bird," Bambi said. "Is that so?"
The yellow thing fluttered its wings and said, "No.

If you had said butterfly, that would be true."
And flapping its wings, off the butterfly flew.

When Bambi leaped over a wildflower bed,
A black-and-white animal poked up its head.

"Look, Thumper!" cried Bambi. "A black-and-white rose,
With small, shiny eyes, and two ears, and a nose!"

"A rose?" giggled Thumper. "Your eyesight is punk.
This isn't a rose—it is Flower the skunk."

"Hi, Flower," called Bambi. "I'm happy to meet you."
"I'll race you," said Flower. "And I'll bet I can beat you!"

"You're silly," said Thumper. "You're just a big talker.
We move very fast—but you're only a walker."

A little while later they stopped in the shade,
And Bambi said, "Thumper, I'm really afraid!
I think we are lost in the forest, don't you?"
"Our friends," answered Thumper, "will help us get through.

They waved to the bumblebees buzzing on blossoms,
And shouted, "Hi, fellows!"

To foxes and possums.

They greeted the bobolinks,

Field mice,

And loons,

Doodlebugs,

Porcupines,

Owls,

And raccoons.

"Say, possum!" they cried. "Can you show us the trail?"
But possum just snored as she hung by her tail.

The bumblebees bumbled,

The doodlebugs doo'd.

The loons only laughed,

And the owls only hoo'd.

"The owls are supposed to be wise," said the mice.
"Speak nicely to one, and he'll give you advice."

So Bambi spoke nicely to one grumpy owl,
Who answered quite wisely, with rather a growl,
"Run that way, my boy, till you come to a lake.
And there you'll discover the trail you should take.

But hurry! Keep racing as long as there's light.
Or you will be caught in the woods overnight!"
They thanked the wise owl, and as fast as they could,
They started to race to the lake in the wood.

A mole stuck his head out, and stopped the whole race,
When Thumper, not seeing him, stepped on his face.

Then Bambi bent down very close to the mole,
Whose head was still sticking up out of the hole.
"We're sorry," said Bambi. "That was a mistake.
Can you tell us how we can get to the lake?"

The mole cleaned his whiskers,
And blinked at the light,

And not even answering,
Sank out of sight.

A squirrel jumped down from the trunk of a tree.
He said, "I can tell you. Just leave it to me.
Stop wondering which of the trails you should take.
Just follow your nose, and you'll come to the lake."

And since that was all he could take time to say,
He picked up an acorn, and hurried away.

They followed their noses, and raced on ahead.
And there was the lake—as the squirrel had said.

On top of a lily pad almost unseen,
Sat something quite lumpy, and shiny, and green.

Said Bambi, "What are you?" And leaped to a log.
The lumpy thing answered, "REE-DEEP! I'm a frog!"

"We're lost," Bambi said. "Can you show us the way?"

"REE-DEEP!" said the frog. And that's all he would say.

The frog's twenty cousins, nine sons, and a daughter,
Swam up to the top—and jumped out of the water.

All over the lake there were frogs by the heap,
All jumping, and splashing, and croaking, "REE-DEEP!"

Just then a young otter
　　Took Bambi aside,
And showed him a mud bank
　　Where otters could slide.

"I'd love to watch longer," said Bambi. "You're great.
But we must go home for it's getting quite late.
We're lost and we know it. Which way should we go?
Just how can we find our way home—do you know?"

"Of course," said the otter.
"It's easy as pie.
Just follow this brook,
And you'll be there—good-by."

So Bambi kept running, and Thumper kept hopping.
The two tired friends hurried home without stopping.

Some fish swam beside them, and cried to each other,
"Hooray—Bambi's found the way home to his mother!"

His mother, at home, had been worried and missed them.
But now she was happy, and hugged them, and kissed them.
"Although we were lost we are home," Bambi said.
"I thought I would never see you or my bed."

"That's silly," said Thumper. "You're only a kid.
I told you I'd get you back home—and I did!"

That night in his home in the wood, dark and deep,
As Bambi was dreaming, he said in his sleep:

"A fish is a swimmer,

An otter's a slider,

A bear is a climber,

A bird is a glider,

A skunk is a walker,

A frog is a jumper,

And also a hopper,
like our little Thumper."